THE ADVENTURES OF THE GRAND VIZIER
BY GOSCINNY & TABARY

IZNOGOUD

I WANT TO BE CALIPH INSTEAD OF THE CALIPH

SCRIPT: RENÉ GOSCINNY   **ARTWORK: JEAN TABARY**

I WANT TO BE CALIPH INSTEAD OF THE CALIPH!

9th **CINEBOOK**
The 9th Art Publisher

'**I want to be caliph instead of the caliph,**' says Iznogoud again and again. This saying is one of René Goscinny's most famous inventions – indeed, it has become a household expression in France.

Iznogoud was born in the pages of Goscinny's illustrated book *Les Vacances du Petit Nicolas* (*Nicholas on Holiday*). In it, a holiday camp monitor tells the children stories of a horrible vizier who's trying to usurp the caliph's throne!

René Goscinny and illustrator Jean Tabary created the character of Iznogoud in 1962. Initially the series was called *The Adventures of Caliph Haroun Al Plassid* and was published in the first issue of magazine *Record*. But the despicable vizier quickly took centre stage and became the titular hero. The duo would co-sign seventeen volumes.

In May 1968, Iznogoud joined Asterix and Lucky Luke, René Goscinny's other characters, in the legendary magazine *Pilote*. Then, from October 1974, Iznogoud became columnist and commented on the news in newspaper *Le Journal du Dimanche*. After the death of René Goscinny in November 1977, Jean Tabary continued to bring Iznogoud's stories to life.

In 2011, the artist joined his writer friend in humorist heaven. But the character of Iznogoud had become so well known that he survived his creators and had – and will continue to have – many more adventures, imagined and illustrated by others.

Original title: Je veux être calife à la place du calife
Original edition: © 2012 IMAV éditions, by Goscinny & Tabary
www.imaveditions.com
www.iznogoud.com
All rights reserved
English translation: © 2016 Cinebook Ltd
Translator: Jerome Saincantin
Lettering and text layout: Design Amorandi
Printed in Spain by EGEDSA
This edition published in Great Britain in 2016 by
Cinebook Ltd
56 Beech Avenue,
Canterbury, Kent
CT4 7TA
www.cinebook.com
A CIP catalogue record for this book
is available from the British Library
ISBN 978-1-84918-310-9

9th CINEBOOK
The 9th Art Publisher

In Baghdad the Magnificent was a grand vizier named Iznogoud. He was very evil and had a single goal in life…

I WANT TO BE CALIPH INSTEAD OF THE CALIPH!!

BE CAREFUL, MASTER.

That despicable vizier had a faithful strong-arm man named Wa'at Alahf – although, with such a boss, he rarely chortled.

Whereas the Caliph of Baghdad, the good **Haroun Al Plassid**, who had absolute confidence in his grand vizier, spent his happy, sleepy days in the sweet serenity of his sovereignty…

Now then, to Baghdad the Magnificent…

IZNOGOUD

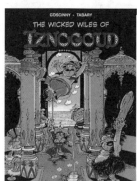

1 - THE WICKED WILES OF IZNOGOUD

2 - THE CALIPH'S VACATION

3 - IZNOGOUD AND THE DAY OF MISRULE

4 - IZNOGOUD AND THE MAGIC COMPUTER

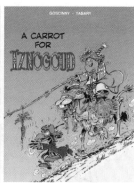

5 - A CARROT FOR IZNOGOUD

6 - IZNOGOUD AND THE MAGIC CARPET

7 - IZNOGOUD THE INFAMOUS

8 - IZNOGOUD ROCKETS TO STARDOM

9 - THE GRAND VIZIER IZNOGOUD

10 - IZNOGOUD THE RELENTLESS

11 - IZNOGOUD AND THE JIGSAW TURK

12 - IZNOGOUD'S FAIRY TALE

13 - I WANT TO BE CALIPH INSTEAD OF THE CALIPH!

COMING SOON

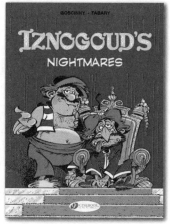

14 - IZNOGOUD'S NIGHTMARES

SOMEWHERE NEAR BAGHDAD THE MAGNIFICENT IS AN ABANDONED OLD PALACE. FEW PEOPLE KNOW THAT THIS SAD PLACE IS HOME TO...

THE INSPECTION SPECTRE

BUT ONE DAY, ATTRACTED BY THE GLOOMY ATMOSPHERE, THE VILE GRAND VIZIER IZNOGOUD CAME TO VISIT THE AREA AND ASKED HIS FAITHFUL STRONG-ARM MAN WA'AT ALAHF THE FOLLOWING QUESTION...

WHAT IS THE STORY OF THIS CHARMING COTTAGE SET IN SUCH A LOVELY SITE?

AND THE FAITHFUL STRONG-ARM MAN ANSWERED...

IT IS THE HOUSE OF THE INSPECTION SPECTRE. LET ME TELL YOU HIS STORY...

...THIS PALACE WAS BUILT A LONG, LONG TIME AGO FOR CALIPH HAN DOVAH AL MOOLAH...

...HE'D HAD IT BUILT THERE BECAUSE THERE WAS NEARBY A SMALL POND FULL OF CARPS, AND THE CALIPH LOVED CARPS...

HERE, FISHY FISHY!

THE CARPS LOVED HIM TOO, AND WHEN THEY HEARD HIM THEY'D COME OUT OF THE MUD TO GREET HIM.

BUT ONE MORNING, WHEN THE CALIPH HAD WALKED TO THE LAKE AS HE WAS WONT TO DO...

HERE, FISHY FISHY FISHY!

...THE CARPS DIDN'T HEED HIS CALL.

WORRIED, THE CALIPH CONDUCTED AN IN-DEPTH INVESTIGATION. DISCOVERING THAT THE POND'S MUD HAD BEEN DISTURBED, HE WAS FORCED TO ACCEPT THE EVIDENCE: THE CARPS HAD DISAPPEARED!

AFTER AN UNDERSTANDABLE MOMENT OF GRIEF, HE CAME TO THE FOLLOWING CONCLUSION...

SOMEONE'S SEIZED MY CARPS!

AND FLYING INTO A VIOLENT RAGE, HE ROARED...

ASSEMBLE THE PALACE GUARDS! I WANT TO INSPECT THEM!

AND DURING THE INSPECTION, HE ASKED...

WHO STUFFED THEMSELVES WITH MY FISH?

STOP! ONE MOMENT!

?

WE INTERRUPT WA'AT ALAHF'S STORY TO MENTION THAT WE COULD ALSO HAVE HAD THE CALIPH SAY...

WHO DEFILED THE FISH POND?

OR EVEN...

WHO GEFILTED MY FISH?

HO! HEY!

CAN I GO BACK TO THE STORY? ARE YOU QUITE DONE WITH YOUR CARPY PUNS?

OH, THOSE TWO! I SWEAR — I'D HAVE THEM IMPALED IF I COULD!...

SO, AS NONE OF THE GUARDS BEING INSPECTED WERE OWNING UP...

...THE CALIPH SAID...

PRESENT YOUR PALMS!

THE GUARDS OBEYED, AND THE CALIPH SAW THAT ONE OF THEM HAD MUD ALL OVER HIS HANDS...

THAT'S WHAT I CALL PAWS-ITIVE IDENTIFICATION!

YEAH! NO MITT-IGATING CIRCUMSTANCES FOR HIM.

THEN THE CALIPH RAISED HIS SCIMITAR AND SAID...

I TAKE A DIEM VIEW OF CARP POACHING!

NOTE FOR THE TRANSLATORS OF THESE BOOKS, WHICH ARE SUCH A MASSIVE SUCCESS WORLDWIDE: THE PRECEDING LINE IS A PUN CENTRED ON THE SHORT-TEMPERED KING OF THE FRANCS CLOVIS. YOU SEE...*

HEY! WILL YOU TWO STOP THAT??!!

JUST AS IT WAS GETTING INTERESTING!

INDEED! BECAUSE OF THIS ABSURD INTERRUPTION, WE'VE MISSED THE BLOODIEST PART OF THIS TALE — ONE THAT COULD FINALLY HAVE MADE US HIP...

ANYWAY, AFTER HAVING CHOPPED OFF THE GUARD'S HEAD, THE CALIPH CALLED AN END TO THE INSPECTION AND, SATISFIED WITH HIS DAY'S WORK, WENT TO BED IN HIS BEAUTIFUL BRAND NEW PALACE.

HEH HEH! THIS SORT OF EMPLOYEE TERMINATION IS SO MUCH SIMPLER!

3

*DEAR READER, LOOK UP 'THE VASE OF SOISSONS' AND COMPARE IT TO 'LA VASE DES POISSONS' (THE FISH'S MUD), IF YOU WANT AN IDEA OF WHAT THEY'RE TALKING ABOUT. BUT OF COURSE, THE ORIGINAL PUN ISN'T INCLUDED HERE, SINCE IT'S IMPOSSIBLE TO TRANSLATE. I NEED SOME ASPIRIN... — THE TRANSLATOR.

WHAT HAPPENED THAT NIGHT? NO ONE TRULY KNOWS. THE FACT IS THAT THE NEXT MORNING, A PANICKED SLAVE CRIED OUT...

COME! COME QUICKLY! THE CALIPH'S GONE GAGA!

I CAME TO BRING HIM HIS BREAKFAST AND I FOUND HIM LIKE THIS!

AGAGA! AGAGA!

YES, THE CALIPH HAD GONE GAGA! IRREPARABLY SENILE. HE SPENT THE REST OF HIS LIFE DOODLING.

AGAGA! AGAGA!

HE WAS REPLACED BY A NEW CALIPH: HASSAN ITARIUM...

...WHO, HAVING TAKEN UP RESIDENCE IN HIS PREDECESSOR'S PALACE, WAS FOUND THIS WAY ON THE FIRST AND LAST DAY OF HIS REIGN...

AGAGA! AGAGA!

HE WAS FOLLOWED BY CALIPH BIN ARUFFDEY...

AGAGA! AGAGA!

...THEN CALIPH MEHMET ROPOLITAN-MUSEUMOFART.

AGAGA! AGAGA!

IN OTHER WORDS, EVERY CALIPH WHO SPENT THE NIGHT IN THIS PALACE BECAME GAGA. PEOPLE THEN FIGURED OUT THAT IT WAS THE GUARD'S GHOST WHO KEPT COMING BACK AND TERRIFYING THE CALIPHS INTO LOOPINESS...

AND SO NO CALIPH EVER SPENT ANOTHER NIGHT IN THIS CURSED PALACE.

WHAT A DELIGHTFUL TALE!

CAN WE VISIT THIS WONDERFUL BUNGALOW?

IF YOU WANT. AS LONG AS YOU'RE NOT A CALIPH, THERE'S NO DANGER.

4

IT'S VERY COSY!

OH? YOU THINK SO?

TELL ME, THOUGH... DO YOU THINK THAT GHOST STORY IS TRUE?

YOU CAN ALWAYS ASK THE GHOST HIMSELF. AS I SAID, HE'S HARMLESS TO NON-CALIPHS.

D'YOU KNOW HOW TO MAKE THE GHOST VISIBLE?

HE JUST NEEDS SOME COLOUR. YOU MAKE A CIRCLE ...

LIKE A MAGIC CIRCLE? DRAWN WITH COLOURED CHALK?

NO. DONE WITH ONIONS.

HE NEEDS TO BE BROWNED WITH ONIONS.

I SHOULD HAVE KNOWN. NOT EVEN SPECTRES HAVE A SHRED OF DIGNITY IN THESE STORIES. LET'S GO AND GET SOME ONIONS.

A LITTLE LATER...

GOOD GRIEF, THAT WASN'T CHEAP! REMIND ME TO FREEZE PRICES ONCE I'M CALIPH INSTEAD OF THE CALIPH!

THERE. PLACE THE ONIONS IN A CIRCLE, THEN SING TO CALL THE GHOST.

SING?

WOOOOOH MY LOOOVE, MY DAAAAARLING, I'VE HUNGERED...

5

ARE... ARE YOU THE INSPECTION SPECTRE?

MMM?

OH YES, SORRY. MY HEAD WAS IN THE CLOUDS... AND WHO ARE YOU TO DARE DISTURB ME? YOU'RE NOT EVEN A CALIPH.

BUT I WANT TO BECOME ONE.

WELL, ONCE YOU DO, NO NEED TO CALL. I'LL COME BACK TO TAKE CARE OF YOU. I ALWAYS COME BACK FOR CALIPHS.

HE ALWAYS COMES BACK FOR CALIPHS! FANTASTIC!

ARE YOU WRONG IN THE HEAD OR SOMETHING?

AND ... WHAT DO YOU DO TO CALIPHS?

THAT'S A SECRET! KNOW THAT WHEN A CALIPH SPENDS THE NIGHT HERE, ON THE TWELFTH STROKE OF MIDNIGHT I RETURN AND MAKE HIM GO OFF HIS HEAD! IT'S MY VENGEANCE!

SO... IF I BROUGHT YOU A CALIPH ... YOU'D MAKE HIM GO SOFT IN THE HEAD?

HEY, MY EYES ARE DOWN HERE, MISTER!

YOU'RE A PIG-HEADED ONE, HUH? LOOK, I WAS VERY CLEAR: YOUR CALIPH WILL BECOME GAGA LIKE THE OTHERS — AS LONG AS HE'S A CALIPH!

RIGHT, GOTTA GO. FOOTBALL GAME TODAY — SPECTRES AGAINST ECTOPLASMS. I PLAY GOALKEEPER.

6

10

WA'AT! THE LAW HASN'T CHANGED, RIGHT? A GAGA CALIPH CAN'T REMAIN CALIPH?

IT HASN'T CHANGED, MASTER, BUT PLEASE...

THEN I'M GOING TO BE CALIPH INSTEAD OF THE CALIPH!

MASTER, DO YOU PREFER WORKING WITH A PENCIL OR A PAINTBRUSH?

?

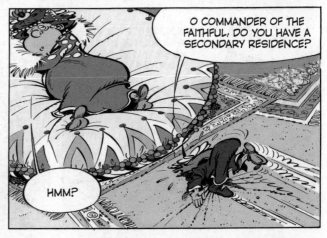

O COMMANDER OF THE FAITHFUL, DO YOU HAVE A SECONDARY RESIDENCE?

HMM?

OF COURSE, MY DEAR IZNOGOUD! I HAVE A PALACE IN EVERY TOWN IN THE CALIPHATE.

NO, NO. I MEAN A HOLIDAY HOME IN THE COUNTRYSIDE... A COTTAGE FOR THE WEEKENDS.

AH, NO!

I HATE THE COUNTRYSIDE. I FIND THE COUNTRYSIDE DEPRESSING. I FIND THE COUNTRYSIDE DREADFULLY DEPRESSING!

SURELY YOU JEST, COMMANDER OF THE FAITHFUL! THINK ABOUT IT: FRESH AIR, FLOWERS, YOUR FRIENDS COMING TO VISIT, CAMEL-MEAT BARBECUES ... ALL JUST 20 MINUTES FROM CENTRAL BAGHDAD.

I BEG OF YOU, COME WITH ME. **FOR ONCE, DO AS I SAY!**

FINE, FINE.

7

?

11

THERE. ONE WORD FROM YOU AND IT'S ALL YOURS.

OH, IS THIS IT?... BUT DON'T PEOPLE TELL SOME SORT OF STORY ABOUT THIS PALACE?...

HOLD ON, I THINK I REMEMBER...

COME NOW! YOU CAN'T GO BELIEVING SUCH POPPYCOCK... LET ME SHOW YOU AROUND YOUR NEW DOMAIN!

GRANTED, IT NEEDS A BIT OF DECORATING... BUT I'LL PAY FOR THE WORK — WITH MY PERSONAL FUNDS.

BUT, YOU KNOW, THE COUNTRYSIDE REALLY DEPRESSES ME AND...

DON'T YOU WORRY. I'LL TAKE CARE OF EVERYTHING. YOU'LL SEE: YOU'LL BE GAGA ABOUT THIS CHALET!

IMMEDIATELY THE TRADESMEN BEGIN WORK, UTTERING THE CORPORATIVE BATTLE CRY...

SORRY, BUT WE'RE GOING TO HAVE TO EXCEED THE ESTIMATE.

AND FOR ONCE, THE HORRIBLE GRAND VIZIER DOESN'T HAGGLE...

IT DOESN'T MATTER. I APPROVE EVERYTHING!

THIS FELLOW'S NUTS!

HE'S ACTUALLY IN A FINE MOOD...

YEAH, WE COULDN'T COME YESTERDAY, AS WE WERE WORKING ON ANOTHER SITE... AND WE'LL HAVE TO EXCEED THE ESTIMATE AGAIN, I'M AFRAID.

NO MATTER, NO MATTER!

YOU'RE GOING BANKRUPT, MASTER.

AS SOON AS I BECOME CALIPH I'LL RAISE NEW TAXES ... AND I'LL HAVE THE BUILDER AND HIS TEAM IMPALED.

8

FINALLY, ONE DAY, A MERE 22 MONTHS AFTER THE ORIGINAL DEADLINE...

BAGHDAD END

THERE, IT'S ALL DONE. THERE ARE A FEW ADDITIONAL FEES...

LET'S HAVE A LOOK!

BAGHDAD END

MAGNIFICENT! MAGNIFICENT!... TOMORROW, ONCE THE CALIPH HAS GONE GAGA, I'LL TEAR DOWN THIS PALACE!

?

?

I DON'T KNOW ABOUT YOU, BUT I FIND THAT THE GRANDEES OF THIS PALACE ARE RATHER UNDIGNIFIED IN THEIR COMINGS AND GOINGS!

WELL?

YES, IT'S NOT BAD. BUT YOU KNOW, THE COUNTRYSIDE...

YES, I KNOW – IT DEPRESSES YOU! SPEND THE NIGHT HERE ANYWAY, AND I SWEAR YOU'LL BE A CHANGED MAN TOMORROW!

SPEND THE NIGHT HERE? TONIGHT?

9

13

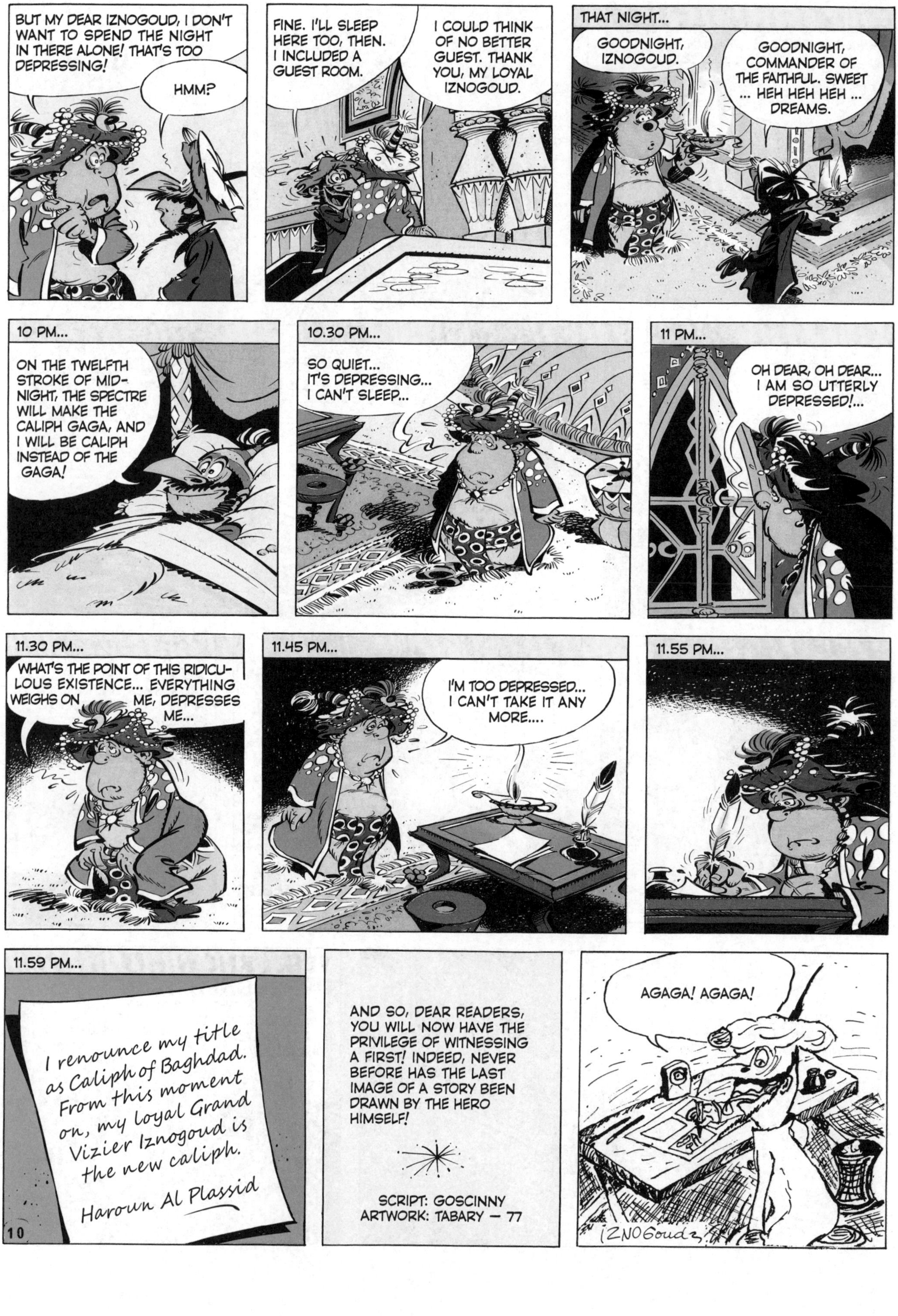
BUT MY DEAR IZNOGOUD, I DON'T WANT TO SPEND THE NIGHT IN THERE ALONE! THAT'S TOO DEPRESSING!
HMM?
FINE. I'LL SLEEP HERE TOO, THEN. I INCLUDED A GUEST ROOM.
I COULD THINK OF NO BETTER GUEST. THANK YOU, MY LOYAL IZNOGOUD.
THAT NIGHT...
GOODNIGHT, IZNOGOUD.
GOODNIGHT, COMMANDER OF THE FAITHFUL. SWEET ... HEH HEH HEH ... DREAMS.
10 PM...
ON THE TWELFTH STROKE OF MID-NIGHT, THE SPECTRE WILL MAKE THE CALIPH GAGA, AND I WILL BE CALIPH INSTEAD OF THE GAGA!
10.30 PM...
SO QUIET... IT'S DEPRESSING... I CAN'T SLEEP...
11 PM...
OH DEAR, OH DEAR... I AM SO UTTERLY DEPRESSED!...
11.30 PM...
WHAT'S THE POINT OF THIS RIDICU-LOUS EXISTENCE... EVERYTHING WEIGHS ON ME, DEPRESSES ME...
11.45 PM...
I'M TOO DEPRESSED... I CAN'T TAKE IT ANY MORE....
11.55 PM...
11.59 PM...
I renounce my title as Caliph of Baghdad. From this moment on, my loyal Grand Vizier Iznogoud is the new caliph.
Haroun Al Plassid
10
AND SO, DEAR READERS, YOU WILL NOW HAVE THE PRIVILEGE OF WITNESSING A FIRST! INDEED, NEVER BEFORE HAS THE LAST IMAGE OF A STORY BEEN DRAWN BY THE HERO HIMSELF!
SCRIPT: GOSCINNY
ARTWORK: TABARY — 77
AGAGA! AGAGA!
IZNOGoud

UNDER THE VIRTUOUS RULE OF THE GOOD HAROUN AL PLASSID, MORALITY AND COMMON DECENCY WERE NOT TO BE TRIFLED WITH IN THE CALIPHATE...

IT'S HIS HAREM. THEY SUSPECT HIM OF BEING SWEET ON ANOTHER HAREM...

...WHICH IS WHY IT MIGHT SOUND BIZARRE — OR EVEN ENTIRELY OUT OF PLACE — THAT THE TITLE OF THIS STORY IS...

SCANDAL IN BAGHDAD

SCRIPT GOSCINNY

ARTWORK TABARY

OH YES, THINGS WERE STRICT IN THE CALIPHATE. IMAGINE, FOR EXAMPLE, THAT TO BECOME A PALACE GUARD, ONE HAD TO PASS MULTIPLE TESTS AND EXAMS.

SNIFF SNIFF SNIFF

SNIFF SNIFF SNIFF... HEH HEH!

?

AND SO, ON THAT DAY, THE VILE GRAND VIZIER IZNOGOUD WAS MEDITATING AS WAS HIS CUSTOM...

I WANT TO BE CALIPH INSTEAD OF THE CALIPH! I WANT TO BE CALIPH INSTEAD OF THE CALIPH!

THAT'S NOT TRUE AT ALL! IT'S NOTHING BUT SLANDER!

???

1

LIES! DISGUSTING FABRICATIONS!

WHO'S MAKING A SCENE?

THIS CHARACTER CLAIMS I GOT MY POSITION AS A GUARD THROUGH NEPOTISM...

NEPOTISM?

ALL RIGHT, SO THE CAPTAIN OF THE GUARDS IS MY COUSIN...

...AND IT'S TRUE I GAVE HIM MONEY. BUT THAT DOESN'T MEAN THAT...

WHAT ARE YOU DOING HERE? WHO ARE YOU?

I'M THE ONE WHO UNEARTHS SCANDALS.

IT'S MY SPECIALITY, ACTUALLY. MY NAME IS LEGUENN-SCANDALES, FROM DISTANT LANDERNEAU.

FOLLOW ME.

YES, NOBLE LORD.

ANYWAY, MY UNCLE THE GENERAL, WHO GOT MY COUSIN HIS POST...

WHAT ABOUT ME? YOU'RE NOT GOING TO BELIEVE THE GOSSIP?

CHIEF OF POLICE! THROW THIS GUARD IN PRISON!

IN PRISON? WHY? WHAT DID MY BROTHER-IN-LAW DO?

?!

BAH, COME ALONG. YOU'LL BE FINE IN PRISON, AFTER ALL. YOUR NEPHEW, THE WARDEN, WILL BE HAPPY TO SEE YOU.

ALL RIGHT, LET'S CUT TO THE CHASE! HOW DID YOU KNOW THAT GUARD OWED HIS POSITION TO A SCANDAL?

I HAVE A MAGICAL GIFT. I CAN SMELL SCANDALS, SNIFF THEM OUT AND EXPOSE THEM!

AND I THOUGHT YOU MIGHT NEED MY SERVICES!

ME?

2

SURE! THERE'S NO BETTER WAY TO TOPPLE A HEAD OF STATE THAN A JUICY SCANDAL!

DO YOU REMEMBER THE FABULOUSLY WEALTHY EMIR BIPI IBN ECKSON AL SHEL, WHO USED TO LIVE IN A PALACE MADE OF GOLD, SILVER AND PLATINUM?...

AFTER I EXPOSED THAT SMALL DECENCY SCANDAL YOU HEARD ABOUT, HE HAD TO STEP DOWN, AND HIS NEW DIGS ARE MUCH SMALLER.

OLD PERVERT

AND PASHA EMONYU, WHO BOUGHT LAND NO ONE WANTED FOR A HANDFUL OF COUSCOUS ...

...AND SOLD IT BACK TO THE THRONE TO BUILD A THALASSOTHERAPY CENTRE IN THE MIDDLE OF THE DESERT?

HE WAS LUCKY TO FIND REFUGE IN A TRADITIONALLY WELCOMING IF DISTANT LAND.

OI! GET A MOVE ON — WE DON'T HAVE TIME TO INVENT THE WHEELBARROW!

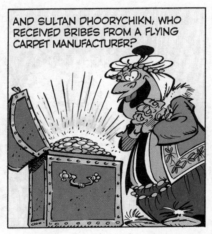
AND SULTAN DHOORYCHIKN, WHO RECEIVED BRIBES FROM A FLYING CARPET MANUFACTURER?

HE HAD TO FLEE THE COUNTRY ON ONE OF THOSE SAME CARPETS.

UNFORTUNATELY FOR HIM, THE CARPETS WEREN'T VERY WELL MADE.

YES, YES, ALL RIGHT. WHAT DOES ANY OF THIS HAVE TO DO WITH ME?

YOU WOULDN'T BY ANY CHANCE WANT TO GET RID OF YOUR HEAD OF STATE TO BECOME HEAD OF STATE INSTEAD OF THE HEAD OF STATE?

3

I'D NEVER THOUGHT ABOUT IT, BUT NOW THAT YOU MENTION IT, WHY NOT?

300,000 DIRHEMS IF IT WORKS.

290,000, AND 25 YEARS IN JAIL IF IT FAILS.

20 YEARS.

DEAL.

NOW I NEED TO TAKE A GOOD SNIFF OF YOUR CALIPH. OBVIOUSLY, IF I DON'T SMELL ANYTHING, OUR CONTRACT IS VOID — BUT THAT WOULD DEFINITELY BE A FIRST...

THIS WAY.

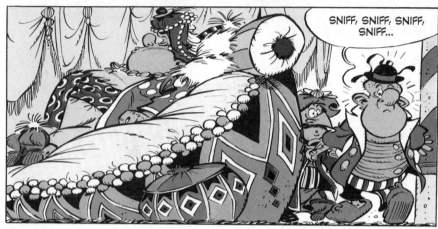

SNIFF, SNIFF, SNIFF, SNIFF...

SNIFF, SNIFF, SNIFF... SNIFF?

COME.

WELL?

UNBELIEVABLE! I COULDN'T SNIFF OUT EVEN A WHIFF OF SCANDAL. THAT GUY IS PURE. WELL, SO LONG THEN, AND NO HARD FEELINGS.

I THOUGHT SO... BUT WITH YOUR EXPERIENCE, COULDN'T YOU MAKE UP SOME SCANDAL?...

MAKE UP A SCANDAL? THAT'S AN ABSOLUTELY SCANDALOUS REQUEST!

IT'S THAT OR IMPALING.

WELL, YOUR ARGUMENT HAS THOROUGHLY SKEWERED MY OBJECTIONS... FINE — BUT I'M NOT SURE IT'LL WORK.

RIGHT. LET'S GO WITH THE USUAL TECHNIQUE: D'YOU HAVE TABLOIDS HERE?

OF COURSE.

DEAR AND PATIENT READERS, YOU ARE OF COURSE AS SURPRISED AS I AM TO HEAR THAT A NEWSPAPER EXISTED IN THOSE ANCIENT TIMES BEFORE GUTENBERG*... BUT DON'T FORGET: BAGHDAD IS A LAND OF MAGIC, AND EVERYTHING IS POSSIBLE THERE, IF NOT PLAUSIBLE.

*JOHANNES GUTENBERG, INVENTOR OF EUROPE'S FIRST PRINTING PRESS IN 1439.

IN ANY CASE...

NEWS IN BRIEF
GO BRIEF THAT...

N°1639 — 2.5 DIRHEMS   FROM 3 TO 9...

Baghdad Sun
52 CITY CENTRE STREET, CLOSE BY

THE CALIPH'S ABANDONED CHILD

FOR YEARS THE CALIPH KEPT HIS TERRIBLE SECRET. "THAT CHILD WAS AN INCONVENIENCE. I SOLD HIM TO SCANDAL DEMAND...

...A LOVE STORY GONE WRONG. THE CHILD WAS SOLD INTO SLAVERY WHEN HE WAS BORN.

FOR YEARS THE CALIPH KEPT HIS TERRIBLE SECRET.

A SCANDAL THAT COULD THREATEN THE THRONE.

"THAT CHILD WAS AN INCONVENIENCE," HE ADMITTED. "I SOLD HIM FOR 12 DIRHEMS."

SO CHEAP? THAT IS A SCANDAL!

IT'S THE TALK OF BAGHDAD. YOUR CALIPH WILL HAVE NO CHOICE BUT TO STEP DOWN.

HE COULD HAVE LIVED IN OPULENCE AS HEIR TO THE THRONE, BUT SURVIVES IN ABJECT MISERY... HA HA! NOT BAD!

SO, THAT'LL BE 290,000 DIRHEMS, AND I'D APPRECIATE IT IF YOU'D KEEP OUR DISHONEST MANOEUVRE A SECRET. I VALUE MY REPUTATION.

LET ME THROUGH! I MUST SEE THE CALIPH!

?

I MUST SEE THE CALIPH!

WHAT'S WITH ALL THE SHOUTING?

WELL, IT'S THAT GUY THERE.

WHY MUST YOU SEE THE CALIPH?

BECAUSE HE'S MY DADDY.

WHAT ?!?!?

THAT'S RIGHT, MISTER! I'M THE CALIPH'S ABANDONED CHILD, AND I CAME BACK TO TAKE MY RIGHTFUL PLACE AS HEIR BY HIS SIDE!

IMPOSTOR!

???

???

5

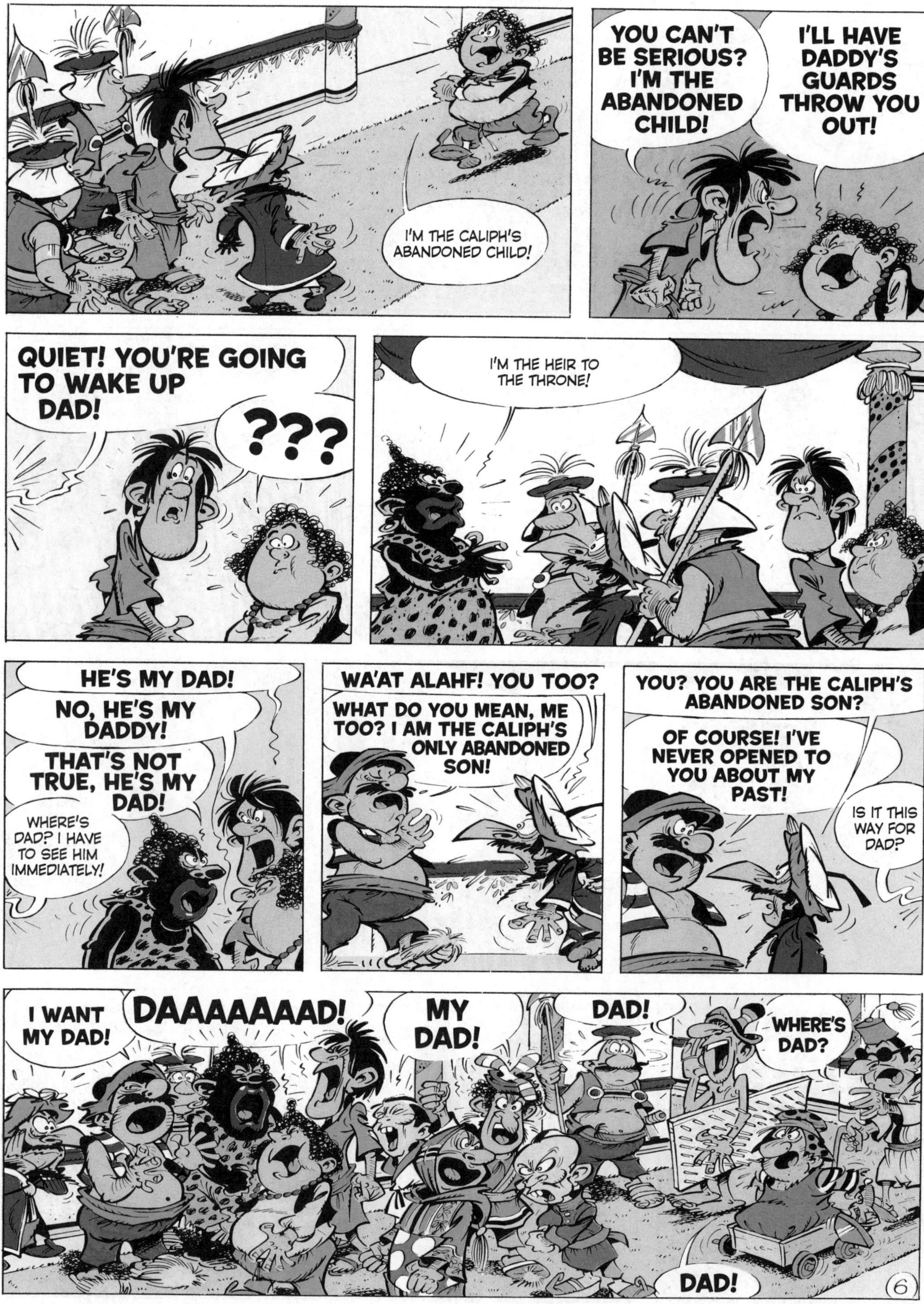
I'M THE CALIPH'S ABANDONED CHILD!
YOU CAN'T BE SERIOUS? I'M THE ABANDONED CHILD!
I'LL HAVE DADDY'S GUARDS THROW YOU OUT!
QUIET! YOU'RE GOING TO WAKE UP DAD!
???
I'M THE HEIR TO THE THRONE!
HE'S MY DAD!
NO, HE'S MY DADDY!
THAT'S NOT TRUE, HE'S MY DAD!
WHERE'S DAD? I HAVE TO SEE HIM IMMEDIATELY!
WA'AT ALAHF! YOU TOO?
WHAT DO YOU MEAN, ME TOO? I AM THE CALIPH'S ONLY ABANDONED SON!
YOU? YOU ARE THE CALIPH'S ABANDONED SON?
OF COURSE! I'VE NEVER OPENED TO YOU ABOUT MY PAST!
IS IT THIS WAY FOR DAD?
I WANT MY DAD!
DAAAAAAAD!
MY DAD!
DAD!
WHERE'S DAD?
DAD!
6

WHAT IS THIS SHOUTING?

WHO DARES TO WAKE ME DURING MY NAP?

DAD!

?!?!?!
?!?

WHY ARE THEY YELLING LIKE THAT, MY DEAR IZNOGOUD?

OH, IT'S QUITE FUNNY: THEY CLAIM TO BE ABANDONED CHILDREN. YOU HAVE TO WONDER WHERE THEY GET SUCH IDEAS, AND...

WHAT? ABANDONED CHILDREN IN BAGHDAD? IT'S A SCANDAL! AND I WILL NOT ABIDE A SCANDAL IN THE CALIPHATE!

I'M ADOPTING THEM ALL. AND NOW TELL THE CHILDREN TO BE QUIET WHILE DADDY GOES BACK TO HIS NAP.

BUT...
BUT?...
HURRAY FOR DAD!

⑦

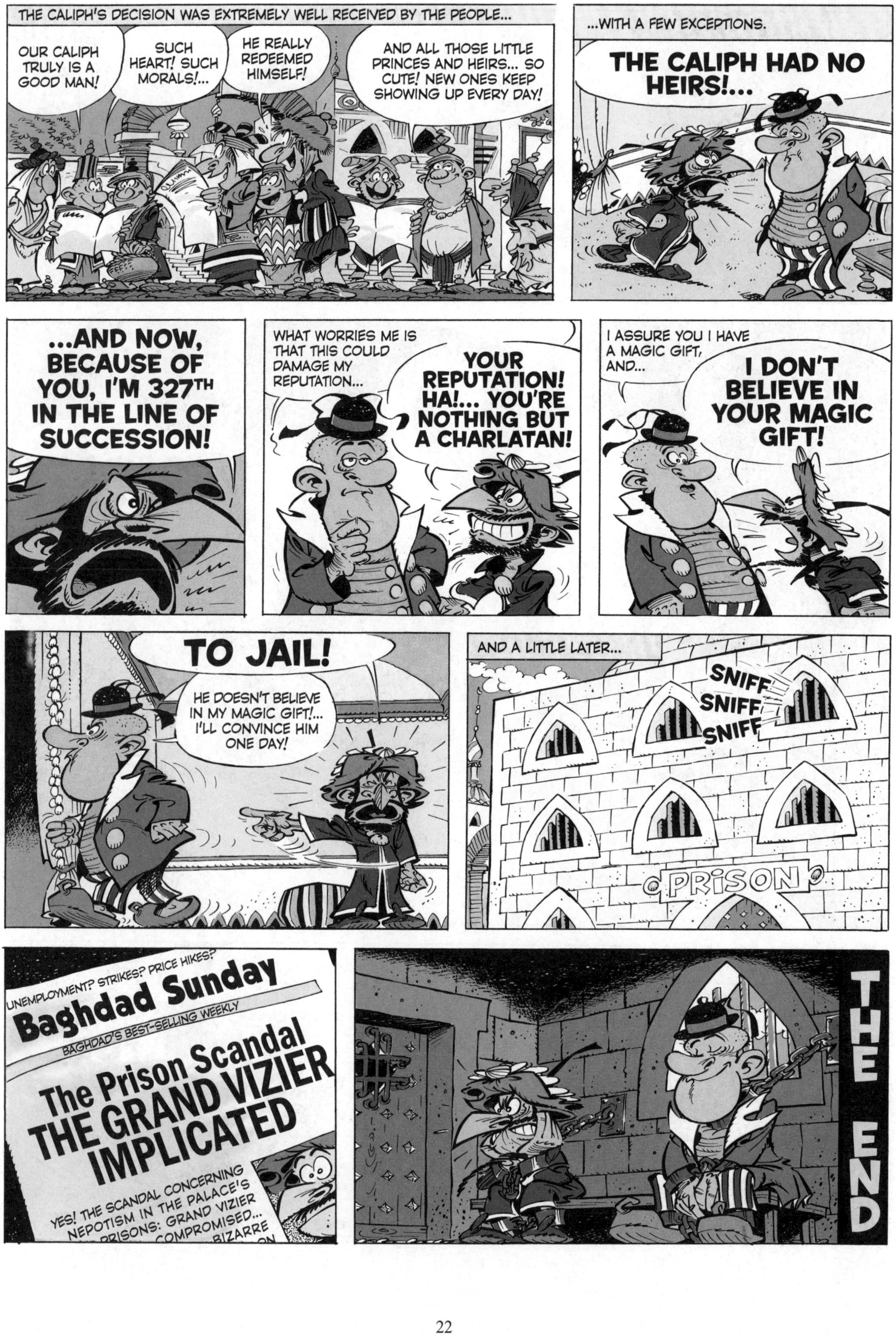
THE CALIPH'S DECISION WAS EXTREMELY WELL RECEIVED BY THE PEOPLE...
OUR CALIPH TRULY IS A GOOD MAN!
SUCH HEART! SUCH MORALS!...
HE REALLY REDEEMED HIMSELF!
AND ALL THOSE LITTLE PRINCES AND HEIRS... SO CUTE! NEW ONES KEEP SHOWING UP EVERY DAY!
...WITH A FEW EXCEPTIONS.
THE CALIPH HAD NO HEIRS!...
...AND NOW, BECAUSE OF YOU, I'M 327TH IN THE LINE OF SUCCESSION!
WHAT WORRIES ME IS THAT THIS COULD DAMAGE MY REPUTATION...
YOUR REPUTATION! HA!... YOU'RE NOTHING BUT A CHARLATAN!
I ASSURE YOU I HAVE A MAGIC GIFT, AND...
I DON'T BELIEVE IN YOUR MAGIC GIFT!
TO JAIL!
HE DOESN'T BELIEVE IN MY MAGIC GIFT!... I'LL CONVINCE HIM ONE DAY!
AND A LITTLE LATER...
SNIFF
SNIFF
SNIFF
PRISON
UNEMPLOYMENT? STRIKES? PRICE HIKES?
Baghdad Sunday
BAGHDAD'S BEST-SELLING WEEKLY
The Prison Scandal
THE GRAND VIZIER IMPLICATED
YES! THE SCANDAL CONCERNING NEPOTISM IN THE PALACE'S PRISONS: GRAND VIZIER COMPROMISED... BIZARRE
THE END

ASIDE FROM PUBLIC EXECUTIONS, THERE ARE FEW CULTURAL ACTIVITIES IN THE CALIPHATE. SO IT'S QUITE AN OCCASION FOR BAGHDAD WHEN SOMEONE OPENS A...

IT IS A GREAT HONOUR FOR ME, O GRAND VIZIER, THAT YOU AGREED TO INAUGURATE MY HUMBLE MUSEUM, WHOSE MODEST FRONT IS GLAD TO SERVE AS THE TITLE OF THIS EPISODE OF YOUR GLORIOUS ADVENTURES.

WAX MUSEUM

ADMITTANCE 10 FALS

LET ME GIVE YOU A TOUR...

ALADDIN AND THE MAGIC LAMP!

HMM...

SINBAD THE SAILOR!

SHEHERAZADE TELLING STORIES TO CALIPH HAROUN AL PLASSID FOR A THOUSAND AND ONE NIGHTS... AND NOW, BETTER AND BETTER...

1

23

...ALI BABA AND THE FORTY THIEVES! IT'S SURREAL HOW LIFELIKE THEY LOOK!

LOOK, FELLOW, HONESTLY...

WAIT, WAIT, YOU HAVEN'T SEEN IT ALL YET. COME...

A LITTLE JOKE IN PASSING: THIS BLOKE HERE IS ACTUALLY A MANNEQUIN...

PEOPLE USUALLY GET IT WRONG.

???

???

AND HERE'S THE HIGHLIGHT OF THE MUSEUM!

KILLERS' ROOM

THE ROOM OF PAST AND FUTURE KILLERS!

PAST AND FUTURE?

OH YES! IT'S THE MAGICAL PART OF MY MUSEUM!

ALL THE MANNEQUINS YOU'RE ABOUT TO SEE REPRESENT THE MOST FEROCIOUS, MOST INFAMOUS ASSASSINS THAT EVER STALKED OR WILL STALK THE EARTH!

HMM...

KILLERS' ROOM

OH! HOW LOVELY!

2

I KNEW YOU'D LIKE IT!

CAN YOU IMAGINE, WA'AT? IF THEY WERE ALIVE, THEY'D HELP ME GET RID OF YOU-KNOW-WHO AND BE YOU-KNOW-WHAT INSTEAD OF YOU-KNOW-WHO.

BUT THERE IS A WAY TO GIVE THEM LIFE, NOBLE GRAND VIZIER!

ARE YOU KIDDING?

I KID YOU NOT! THERE IS A MAGIC SPELL THAT CAN BRING MY WAX MANNEQUINS TO LIFE.

A MAGIC SPELL? WHAT MAGIC SPELL?

IF YOU WANT TO LEARN IT, YOU'LL HAVE TO PAY A LITTLE EXTRA.

MASTER! A WORD.

YES?

NO!

HOW MUCH?

A MILLION DIRHEMS. NO CHEQUES, PLEASE.

ARE YOU SURE 'MONOPOLY' IS THE NEW NAME FOR THE BANK OF BAGHDAD?

SO? THAT MAGIC SPELL?

LOOK THE MANNEQUIN STRAIGHT IN THE EYES AND TELL IT 'WHAT BEAUTIFUL EYES YOU HAVE!'

AND ... CAN I PICK WHICH ONE?

ABSOLUTELY. AS MANY TIMES AS YOU WISH, TOO.

③

ADOPTIVE SON OF JULIUS CAESAR, AND ONE OF HIS ASSASSINS.

26

A HEAD OF STATE? JUST MY THING!

THE PALACE IS JUST ACROSS THE STREET — YOU CAN'T MISS IT.

THIS IS FANTASTIC! THIS MOST EXCELLENT PROFESSIONAL IS GOING TO TAKE CARE OF THE CALIPH FOR ME, AND FINALLY I'LL BE...

?!?   ?!?

WHACKK!

BY JUPITER! THIS CITY OF YOURS IS DANGEROUS! THERE'S SOME THUG OUTSIDE HITTING EVERYONE WITH A CLUB!

BUT YOU'RE AN ASSASSIN! ALL YOU HAVE TO DO IS...

I'M A SPECIALIST IN HEADS OF STATE, SIR! NOT IN CLUB-WIELDING THUGS!

GET BACK OUT THERE! I GAVE YOU LIFE, AFTER ALL!

OH, BECAUSE YOU CALL THIS A LIFE, DO YOU?

THESE ROMANS ARE CRAZY!

WA'AT IS RIGHT. I'LL PICK ANOTHER ONE.

ARE YOU SURE YOU'RE NOT ASTERIX AND OBELIX?

AL CAPONE

AMERICAN GANGSTER AND BOSS OF THE CHICAGO OUTFIT IN THE 1930s.

WHAT BEAUTIFUL EYES YOU HAVE!

I LIKE YOU TOO — YOU DON'T LOOK UNTOUCHABLE.

I NEED A CALIPH REMOVED, BUT THERE'S SOMEONE OUT THERE BLOCKING THE WAY.

LEAVE HIM TO ME.

LISTEN, FELLA. THERE'S NO NEED FOR US TO FIGHT. WE CAN COME TO AN ARRANGEMENT...

GLURK?

I SEE WE UNDERSTAND EACH OTHER. SO LET'S SPLIT THIS TOWN. I'LL TAKE THE NORTH AND LEAVE YOU THE SOUTH...

CIGAR?

GLURK!

WHACKK!

!?!

THAT WISE GUY WANTS A WAR... WAKE UP MY GANG!

YOUR GANG?

YEAH, THOSE FELLAS OVER THERE.

AH...

WHAT... WHAT BEAUTIFUL EYES YOU ALL HAVE!

FRANK THE KNIFE

PISTOL JOE

ILLA

CANNON SAM

MACHIN GUN-LOU

OK, BOYS! THERE'S A GANG THAT NEEDS BRINGING TO HEEL. FOLLOW ME!

OK, BOSS!

BUT... THE CALIPH?

FIRST THE OPPOSITION, FELLA!

6

I'LL TRY ANOTHER ONE...

LANDRU

GOOD GRIEF. IT'S GETTING INCREASINGLY HARDER TO SAY... ANYWAY, HERE GOES!

FRENCH SERIAL KILLER FROM THE EARLY 20TH CENTURY, KNOWN FOR GETTING RID OF HIS VICTIMS' BODIES IN HIS STOVE.

WHAT BEAUTIFUL EYES YOU HAVE!

YOU'RE NOT THE FIRST ONE TO SAY SO.

SO, I NEED YOU TO KILL ONE FAT, HARMLESS GUY...

A GENTLEMAN? BUT I ONLY DEAL WITH LADIES. IF THERE'S A LADY YOU NEED TO DISPOSE OF, THEN I...

LADIES HAVE ABSOLUTELY NOTHING TO DO WITH THIS STORY!

HOW DREADFUL! A MISOGYNIST!

THAT'S TRUE, THEY'VE OFTEN BEEN ACCUSED OF MISOGYNY.

WHO?

LOOK...

WELL, THEM! ASTERIX AND OBELIX.

DO YOU MIND?...

OH! SUCH SPLENDOUR!

LUCREZIA BORGIA

THIS FACE... THESE EYES... OH, THESE EYES!...

ARE YOU EVEN LISTENING TO ME?

WHAT BEAUTIFUL EYES YOU HAVE!

NO-O-O-O-O-O!

7

A MEMBER OF THE POWERFUL BORGIA FAMILY DURING THE ITALIAN RENAISSANCE, SHE IS RUMOURED TO HAVE BEEN A SERIAL POISONER.

YOU'RE NOT SO BAD YOURSELF, O BEARDED ONE!

HEY! IT COSTS A MILLION DIRHEMS TO USE THE MAGIC SPELL, AND...

IT'S TOO NOISY HERE... WHY DON'T WE FIND A QUIET SPOT TO HAVE DINNER?

GLADLY!

I'M VERY GOOD WITH A STOVE.

AND I'LL MAKE YOU ONE OF MY TRADEMARK COCKTAILS!

WHAT... WHAT IS WRONG WITH THIS PACK OF LUNATICS?

NOW SEE HERE, MY LITTLE GAUL! YOU MAY BE A SOCIAL PHENOMENON, BUT THAT DOES NOT GIVE YOU THE RIGHT TO...

OH, GET OUT OF HERE, YOU!

FINE, FINE. AVE!

YOU HAVE TO ADMIT THEY WERE MORE MALLEABLE WHEN THEY WERE MADE OF WAX, WEREN'T THEY?

AND YOU – I WANT A REFUND! I DIDN'T COMPLIMENT THEIR EYES BECAUSE THEY WERE EASY ON MINE!

THAT'S OUT OF THE QUESTION – NOR IS IT IT!

WE'D LIKE TO INTERRUPT THE ACTION FOR A MOMENT AND GIVE YOU TIME TO FULLY APPRECIATE THE CONSTRUCTION OF THIS LAST EXCHANGE, WHICH, AS FAR AS WE KNOW, IS A FIRST.

THE QUESTION, MY GOOD SIR, IS THAT IT'S ALMOST 7 PM, AND IF YOU DON'T BRING BACK ALL MY CHARGES, YOU'LL BE TURNED INTO A WAX MANNEQUIN TOO...

WHAT ?!?!?

YES. AND NO MAGIC SPELL CAN EVER BRING YOU BACK TO LIFE THEN. SO YOU'D BETTER HURRY. TOODLE-OO.

WA'AT! WA'AT ALAHF! HELP ME BRING THEM ALL BACK! WA'AT!

8

WHERE'S HE GONE NOW? NEVER HERE WHEN YOU NEED HIM, THAT ONE!

30

INDEED, WHERE IS THE FAITHFUL WA'AT ALAHF?

IT'S A QUALITY ITEM THAT WILL LAST A LIFETIME.

RATATATATA TATA

BANG!

BANG!

BANG!

BANG!

YOU NEED TO RETURN TO THE MUSEUM RIGHT AWAY!

CAN'T YOU SEE I'M BUSY?

HALF MY GANG BETRAYED ME TO FOLLOW THE FOOL WITH THE CLUB!

I'M WILLING TO GO BACK IF HE DOES TOO! THERE'S NO WAY I'M LETTING HIM HAVE THIS CITY. I HAVE A REPUTATION TO UPHOLD!

I'LL TALK TO HIM!

BANG!

BANG!

BANG!

BANG!

QUICK! YOU MUST GO BACK! I'LL EXPLAIN LATER!

GLURK?

WHACKK!

9

AND WHILE THE MANNEQUINS LIVE THEIR OWN LIVES, FREED FROM ALL CONSTRAINT...

ALMOST READY! THE STOVE'S ALL FIRED UP!

AND I'VE PREPARED YOUR COCKTAIL...

...WELL, ALMOST ALL CONSTRAINT...

WHAT DO YOU MEAN, PUBLIC INDECENCY? WHAT DO YOU MEAN, NAKED IN A BED SHEET? IT'S A TOGA, YOU IGNORA-MUSES! A TOGA!

...AND BRING SOME LIFE TO THE STREETS OF PEACEFUL BAGHDAD...

BANG!

BANG!

BANG!

BANG!

RATATATAT!

BANG!

WHACKK!

SEVEN O'CLOCK COMES...

IT'S SEVEN O'CLOCK - MUSEUMS ARE CLOSING!

WITH WHAT I HAVE TO SHOW NOW, I'LL HAVE TO LOWER MY PRICES.

ADMITTANCE 5 FALS

10

...AND ALL IS WELL AGAIN!

IZNOGOUD

THE VORACIOUS CUSHION

SCRIPT AND ARTWORK: TABARY

HERE'S THE TEXT OF MY AD: 'GRAND VIZIER SEEKS SURE-FIRE WAY TO BECOME CALIPH INSTEAD OF THE CALIPH. BIG REWARD.' CLEAR, ISN'T IT?

TOO CLEAR!...

...WHAT IF SOMEONE WERE TO SHOW IT TO THE CALIPH?...

YOU, PERHAPS? YOU'RE RIGHT. I NEED A TEXT THAT DOESN'T POINT TO ME... I KNOW!

I'M GOING TO MAKE IT: 'WA'AT ALAHF, FAITHFUL STRONG-ARM MAN, SEEKS SURE-FIRE WAY TO GET RID OF GRAND VIZIER AND TAKE HIS PLACE'. YOU'LL PASS ON THE SUGGESTIONS YOU RECEIVE TO ME!

BUT... MASTER...

RESIGNED TONE.

A FEW DAYS LATER...

SO?

HUNDREDS OF LETTERS, MASTER! IT'S INCREDIBLE HOW MANY PEOPLE WOULD LIKE TO SEE YOU GONE!

BUT AT THAT MOMENT, AT THE PALACE ENTRANCE...

I'M HERE TO SEE THE GRAND VIZIER, PLEASE.

YOU MUST BE MAD!...

...BUT IT TAKE ALL KINDS. TAKE STAIRCASE B. ON THE 3RD FLOOR FOLLOW THE CORRIDOR, TAKE A LEFT, THEN RIGHT, THEN THE MIDDLE! 4TH DOOR ON THE LEFT, LOOK ON THE WALL OPPOSITE IT. THERE'S A PLAN OF THE PALACE THAT'LL SHOW YOU WHERE TO GO.

THEY ALL GIVE THE SAME ADVICE, MASTER... LET THE CALIPH KNOW WHAT A VILE PERSON YOU ARE! AND THE DESPICABLE GOAL YOU'RE PURSUING! THE PROOF OF WHICH CAN BE FOUND IN THE 12 VOLUMES ALREADY PUBLISHED BY...

IF YOU DO THAT, I'LL HAVE YOU IMPALED! TRAITOR!!

YOU'D GO THE SAME WAY, MASTER!

THE NEXT DAY...

MASTER, THERE'S A TIRED MAN CARRYING TWO SUITCASES ASKING TO SEE YOU.

HOW STRANGE.

MY GOODNESS! IT'S AN ADVENTURE TO SEEK YOU OUT!

YES, BUT SEEK AND YE SHALL FIND. WHAT'S THIS ABOUT?

I'M HERE ABOUT THE AD YOU PLACED IN THE EVENING BAGHDAD. I HAVE WHAT YOU NEED TO BE CALIPH INSTEAD OF THE CALIPH!

NO KIDDING?

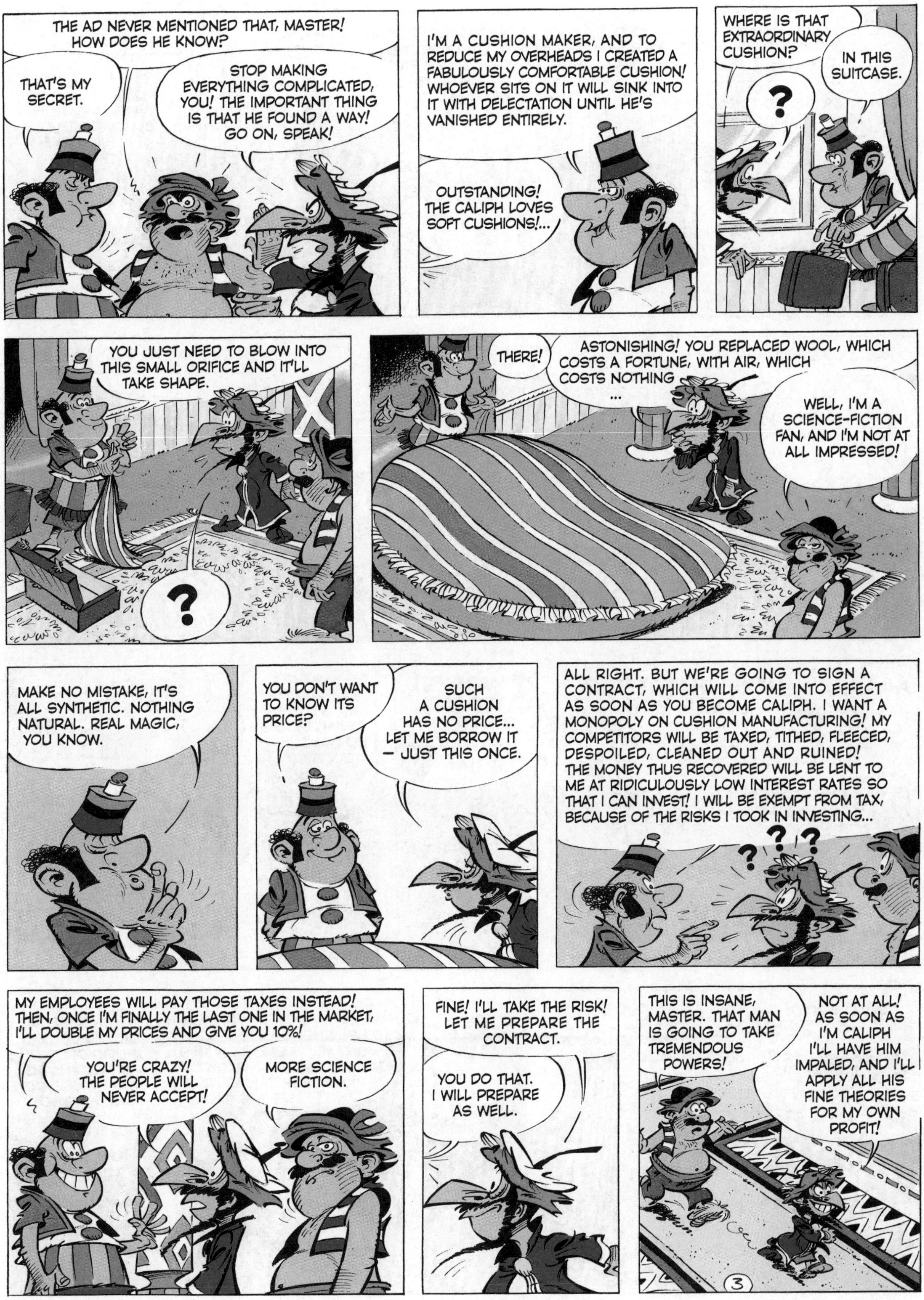

THE AD NEVER MENTIONED THAT, MASTER! HOW DOES HE KNOW?
THAT'S MY SECRET.
STOP MAKING EVERYTHING COMPLICATED, YOU! THE IMPORTANT THING IS THAT HE FOUND A WAY! GO ON, SPEAK!
I'M A CUSHION MAKER, AND TO REDUCE MY OVERHEADS I CREATED A FABULOUSLY COMFORTABLE CUSHION! WHOEVER SITS ON IT WILL SINK INTO IT WITH DELECTATION UNTIL HE'S VANISHED ENTIRELY.
OUTSTANDING! THE CALIPH LOVES SOFT CUSHIONS!...
WHERE IS THAT EXTRAORDINARY CUSHION?
IN THIS SUITCASE.
?
YOU JUST NEED TO BLOW INTO THIS SMALL ORIFICE AND IT'LL TAKE SHAPE.
?
THERE!
ASTONISHING! YOU REPLACED WOOL, WHICH COSTS A FORTUNE, WITH AIR, WHICH COSTS NOTHING ...
WELL, I'M A SCIENCE-FICTION FAN, AND I'M NOT AT ALL IMPRESSED!
MAKE NO MISTAKE, IT'S ALL SYNTHETIC. NOTHING NATURAL. REAL MAGIC, YOU KNOW.
YOU DON'T WANT TO KNOW ITS PRICE?
SUCH A CUSHION HAS NO PRICE... LET ME BORROW IT – JUST THIS ONCE.
ALL RIGHT. BUT WE'RE GOING TO SIGN A CONTRACT, WHICH WILL COME INTO EFFECT AS SOON AS YOU BECOME CALIPH. I WANT A MONOPOLY ON CUSHION MANUFACTURING! MY COMPETITORS WILL BE TAXED, TITHED, FLEECED, DESPOILED, CLEANED OUT AND RUINED! THE MONEY THUS RECOVERED WILL BE LENT TO ME AT RIDICULOUSLY LOW INTEREST RATES SO THAT I CAN INVEST! I WILL BE EXEMPT FROM TAX, BECAUSE OF THE RISKS I TOOK IN INVESTING...
? ? ?
MY EMPLOYEES WILL PAY THOSE TAXES INSTEAD! THEN, ONCE I'M FINALLY THE LAST ONE IN THE MARKET, I'LL DOUBLE MY PRICES AND GIVE YOU 10%!
YOU'RE CRAZY! THE PEOPLE WILL NEVER ACCEPT!
MORE SCIENCE FICTION.
FINE! I'LL TAKE THE RISK! LET ME PREPARE THE CONTRACT.
YOU DO THAT. I WILL PREPARE AS WELL.
THIS IS INSANE, MASTER. THAT MAN IS GOING TO TAKE TREMENDOUS POWERS!
NOT AT ALL! AS SOON AS I'M CALIPH I'LL HAVE HIM IMPALED, AND I'LL APPLY ALL HIS FINE THEORIES FOR MY OWN PROFIT!
3

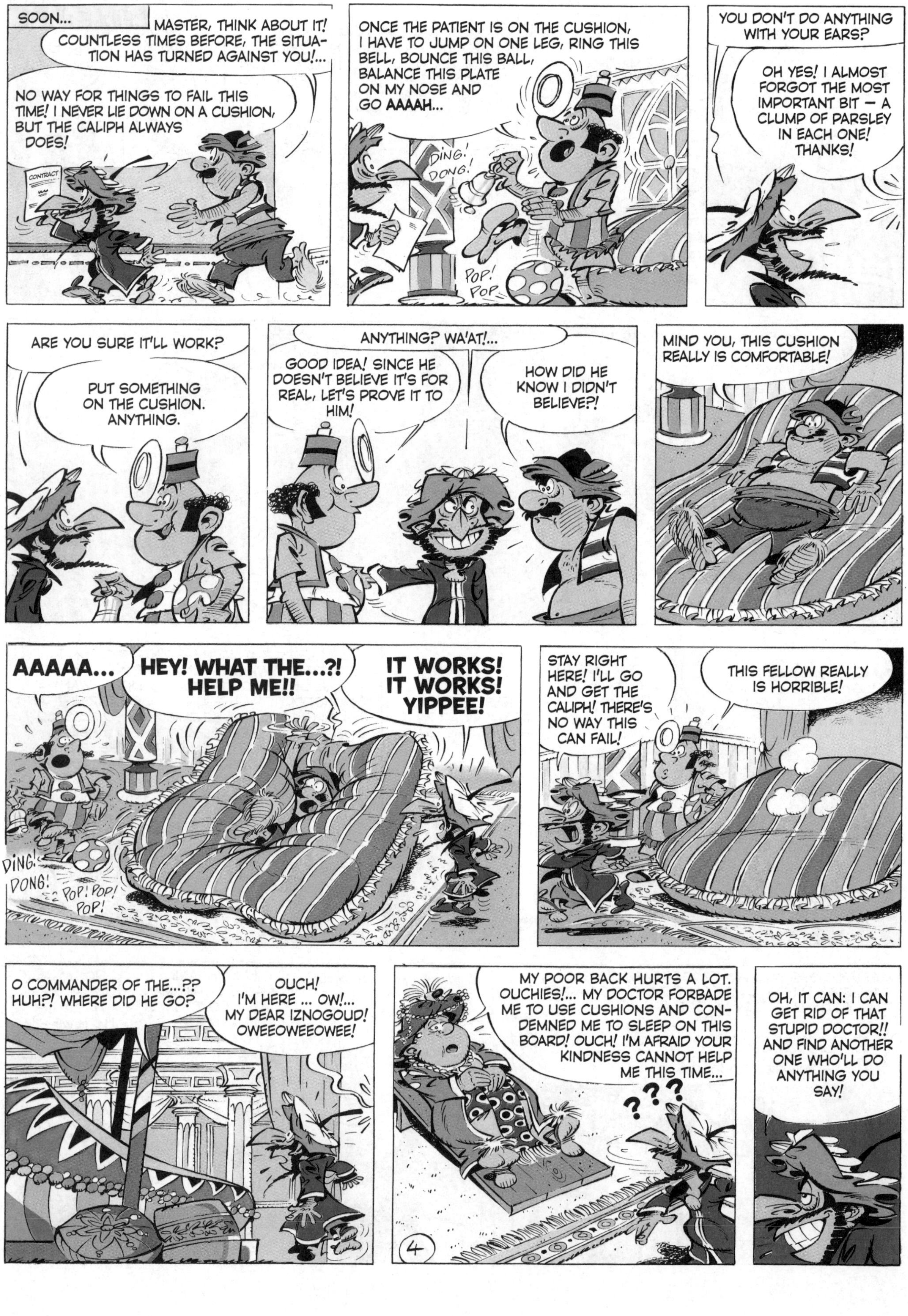
SOON...
MASTER, THINK ABOUT IT! COUNTLESS TIMES BEFORE, THE SITUATION HAS TURNED AGAINST YOU!...
NO WAY FOR THINGS TO FAIL THIS TIME! I NEVER LIE DOWN ON A CUSHION, BUT THE CALIPH ALWAYS DOES!
CONTRACT
ONCE THE PATIENT IS ON THE CUSHION, I HAVE TO JUMP ON ONE LEG, RING THIS BELL, BOUNCE THIS BALL, BALANCE THIS PLATE ON MY NOSE AND GO **AAAAH**...
DING! DONG!
POP! POP!
YOU DON'T DO ANYTHING WITH YOUR EARS?
OH YES! I ALMOST FORGOT THE MOST IMPORTANT BIT — A CLUMP OF PARSLEY IN EACH ONE! THANKS!
ARE YOU SURE IT'LL WORK?
PUT SOMETHING ON THE CUSHION. ANYTHING.
ANYTHING? WA'AT!...
GOOD IDEA! SINCE HE DOESN'T BELIEVE IT'S FOR REAL, LET'S PROVE IT TO HIM!
HOW DID HE KNOW I DIDN'T BELIEVE?!
MIND YOU, THIS CUSHION REALLY IS COMFORTABLE!
AAAAA...
HEY! WHAT THE...?! HELP ME!!
IT WORKS! IT WORKS! YIPPEE!
DING! DONG!
POP! POP! POP!
STAY RIGHT HERE! I'LL GO AND GET THE CALIPH! THERE'S NO WAY THIS CAN FAIL!
THIS FELLOW REALLY IS HORRIBLE!
O COMMANDER OF THE...?? HUH?! WHERE DID HE GO?
OUCH! I'M HERE ... OW!... MY DEAR IZNOGOUD! OWEEOWEEOWEE!
MY POOR BACK HURTS A LOT. OUCHIES!... MY DOCTOR FORBADE ME TO USE CUSHIONS AND CONDEMNED ME TO SLEEP ON THIS BOARD! OUCH! I'M AFRAID YOUR KINDNESS CANNOT HELP ME THIS TIME...
???
4
OH, IT CAN: I CAN GET RID OF THAT STUPID DOCTOR!! AND FIND ANOTHER ONE WHO'LL DO ANYTHING YOU SAY!

IN THE MEANTIME, WHY DON'T WE PUT THIS BOARD ON A CUSHION? IT'LL BE MORE COMFORTABLE THAT WAY!

DO YOU THINK SO, MY DEAR IZNOGOUD?

I'M SURE — FOR THE PLANK, IF NOTHING ELSE!

WAIT FOR ME ... OUCH! MY POOR BACK! OW! OW! OW!

HEY, MR ONE-MAN-BAND!? GET READY — HE'S COMING!

? AAAA...

DING! DONG! POP! POP! POP!

AAAAA... AAHHH!

DING! DONG! DING! POP! POP! POP!

THERE! TO THINK THAT NASTY LITTLE MAN MEANT TO HAVE ME IMPALED!!

HAVE YOU SEEN A SMALL, FRIENDLY LOOKING MAN CARRYING A BOARD, BY ANY CHANCE? HE'S MY GRAND VIZIER. I'M LOOKING FOR HIM...

ARE YOU THE CALIPH?

COULD YOU TELL ME IF THIS CONTRACT IS VALID? IT'S SIGNED BY YOUR GRAND VIZIER IZNOGOUD.

ANYTHING SIGNED BY MY DEAR IZNOGOUD IS SACRED. THAT MAN THINKS OF NOTHING BUT THE GOOD OF HIS COUNTRY, ITS PEOPLE AND ITS CALIPH.

PERFECT, THEN! I'LL PACK UP AND GO!

YOO-HOO! MY DEAR IZNOGOUD?! NOW'S NOT THE TIME TO PLAY HIDE AND SEEK WITH MY BOARD. MY POOR BACK HURTS...

I NEED TO HURRY, OR HE'LL ARRIVE BEFORE ME AND WONDER WHERE HE IS.

HE'S RUNNING OUT — THAT MEANS HE MET HIM.

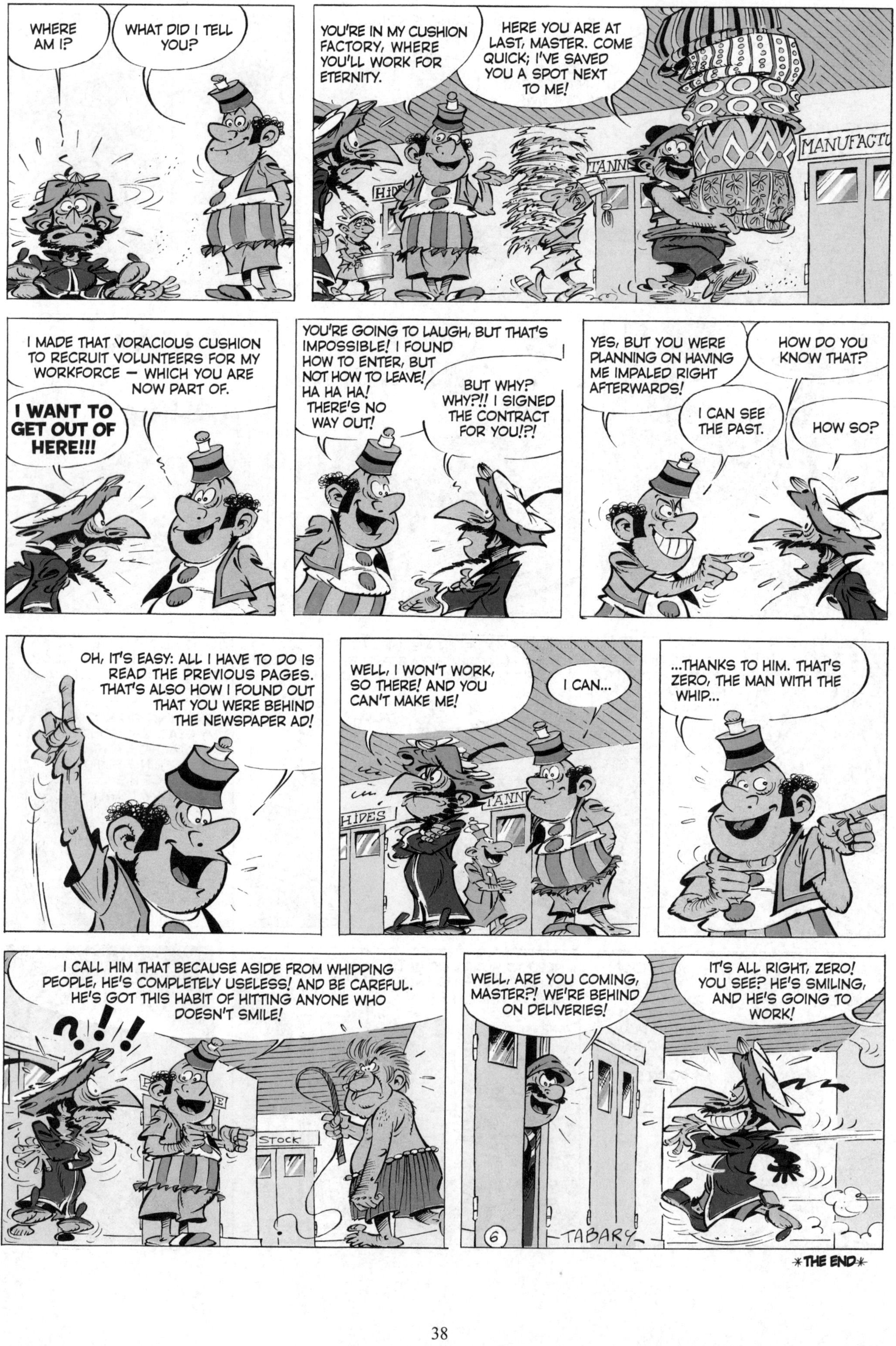

WHERE AM I?
WHAT DID I TELL YOU?
YOU'RE IN MY CUSHION FACTORY, WHERE YOU'LL WORK FOR ETERNITY.
HERE YOU ARE AT LAST, MASTER. COME QUICK; I'VE SAVED YOU A SPOT NEXT TO ME!
HIDES
TANN
MANUFACTU
I MADE THAT VORACIOUS CUSHION TO RECRUIT VOLUNTEERS FOR MY WORKFORCE — WHICH YOU ARE NOW PART OF.
I WANT TO GET OUT OF HERE!!!
YOU'RE GOING TO LAUGH, BUT THAT'S IMPOSSIBLE! I FOUND HOW TO ENTER, BUT NOT HOW TO LEAVE! HA HA HA! THERE'S NO WAY OUT!
BUT WHY? WHY?!! I SIGNED THE CONTRACT FOR YOU!?!
YES, BUT YOU WERE PLANNING ON HAVING ME IMPALED RIGHT AFTERWARDS!
HOW DO YOU KNOW THAT?
I CAN SEE THE PAST.
HOW SO?
OH, IT'S EASY: ALL I HAVE TO DO IS READ THE PREVIOUS PAGES. THAT'S ALSO HOW I FOUND OUT THAT YOU WERE BEHIND THE NEWSPAPER AD!
WELL, I WON'T WORK, SO THERE! AND YOU CAN'T MAKE ME!
I CAN...
HIDES
TANN
...THANKS TO HIM. THAT'S ZERO, THE MAN WITH THE WHIP...
I CALL HIM THAT BECAUSE ASIDE FROM WHIPPING PEOPLE, HE'S COMPLETELY USELESS! AND BE CAREFUL. HE'S GOT THIS HABIT OF HITTING ANYONE WHO DOESN'T SMILE!
?!!
STOCK
WELL, ARE YOU COMING, MASTER?! WE'RE BEHIND ON DELIVERIES!
IT'S ALL RIGHT, ZERO! YOU SEE? HE'S SMILING, AND HE'S GOING TO WORK!
6
TABARY

THE END

THE CALIPHAL ARMY IS MADE-UP OF MERCENARIES PAID DIRECTLY BY HAROUN AL PLASSID, THE GENTLE CALIPH OF BAGHDAD. ONCE A YEAR, THE CEREMONY OF CONTRACT RENEWAL BY TACIT AGREEMENT TAKES PLACE. IT IS WITH THIS MARTIAL YET MOVING RITUAL THAT BEGINS OUR STORY, WHICH BEARS THE NAME...

THE EGGS OF UR

SCRIPT: GOSCINNY. ARTWORK: TABARY

NOW COMES THE TIME FOR THE OATH TAKING BY THE ARMY'S GENERAL-IN-CHIEF ARASH UNPAK...

AHEM...

WE HEREBY SWEAR FEALTY TO THE CALIPH, HEREAFTER REFERRED TO AS 'THE CLIENT', AND DECLARE WE ARE WILLING TO FIGHT TO THE DEATH FOR HIM UNTIL NEXT YEAR, SAME DATE...

...BARRING THE SENDING OF A RECORDED LETTER DENOUNCING THE CONTRACT BEFORE ITS EXPIRATION (PARAGRAPH 2).

IT'S SO MOVING, MY DEAR IZNOGOUD!

ANNEX A: WHILE THE CONTRACT IS VALID, WE SWEAR TO NEUTRALISE ANYONE WHO WOULD DARE TO PLOT AGAINST THE CLIENT!

1

OFFICERS, NON-COMMISSIONED OFFICERS AND ENLISTED MEN! TAKE YOUR OATH!

READ AND APPROVED, SIGNED AND AGREED!!!

IT'S OUR TURN... DO YOU HAVE IT?

YES, O COMMANDER OF THE FAITHFUL.

10, 20, 30, 40 AND 50 MILLION.

THEN COMES A MINUTE OF DIGNIFIED SILENCE...

...UNTIL, AT LAST, A BRIEF ORDER SOUNDS THE END OF THE PARADE.

IT'S ALL THERE!

THIS YEAR, HOWEVER, SEVERAL DAYS BEFORE THE PREVIOUSLY DESCRIBED CEREMONY IS SCHEDULED TO TAKE PLACE, IN BAGHDAD'S FANCIEST RESTAURANT...

LE MINARET D'ARGENT

YOU'RE NOT EATING, MASTER? THIS GREEN PEPPER ELEPHANT IS DELICIOUS!

THE ARMY!... THAT'S THE CALIPHAL THRONE'S BEST SUPPORT...

IF I HAD THE ARMY IN MY POCKET, IT'D HELP ME TOPPLE THE CALIPH, AND I'D BECOME CALIPH INSTEAD OF THE CALIPH...

②

YOUR ELEPHANT À L'ORANGE MUST BE VERY GOOD, TOO...

I DISCUSSED IT WITH GENERAL ARASH UNPAK. FOR 60 MILLION, HE'D SIGN UP WITH ME IMMEDIATELY...

...BUT WHERE COULD I FIND SUCH A SUM?

OH, MY GOODNESS!

WHO IS THAT SHABBY WRETCH?

THAT'S NOKATSH THE FISHERMAN, THE POOREST MAN IN BAGHDAD.

YOU! I DEMAND YOU IMMEDIATELY...

ONE MOMENT.

IT'S PURE GOLD. WILL THAT BE ENOUGH FOR A MEAL?

...FOLLOW ME?

MAKE IT A NICE TABLE, PLEASE.

DID... DID YOU SEE THAT???

WAS IT TO SIR'S SATISFACTION?

YEAH, NOT BAD. I'M BUYING THE RESTAURANT.

TOMORROW WE'LL RAISE THE PRICES. I WOULDN'T WANT LOSERS LIKE ME COMING INTO MY PLACE ANY MORE.

YES, BOSS. SEE YOU TOMORROW, BOSS.

WA'AT! GO AFTER HIM AND BRING HIM TO ME AT THE PALACE!

3

41

SOON...

THIS PALACE ISN'T BAD... I'LL BUY IT IF YOU'RE SELLING.

I WANT AN EXPLANATION: HOW DID YOU BECOME SO RICH WHEN YOU WERE THE POOREST OF FISHERMEN?

THAT'S THE THING, OLD FELLOW. I'VE BECOME SUFFICIENTLY RICH THAT I DON'T HAVE TO ANSWER YOUR QUESTIONS.

IS THAT SO?

KNOW THEN, MY FRIEND, THAT BEING FLUSH WITH DIRHEMS WON'T PROTECT YOU FROM IMPALING.

I DISCOVERED A TREASURE.

A TREASURE? WHAT TREASURE?

THE OSTRICH WITH THE GOLDEN EGGS!

HUH?

HERE'S WHAT HAPPENED. I WAS SAILING DOWN THE TIGRIS IN MY BOAT, LOOKING FOR THE CATFISH THAT MAKE UP MOST OF MY MEAGRE FARE...

TIRED AFTER AN UNSUCCESSFUL DAY THAT HAD STARTED AT FIRST LIGHT, I DECIDED TO BREAK UP THE ROUTINE AND GO ASHORE FOR A WHILE... MY FEET TOOK ME TO THE ANCIENT CITY OF UR...

AND THAT'S WHERE I FOUND THE OSTRICH WITH THE GOLDEN EGGS, AND IT WAS KIND ENOUGH TO LAY A FEW DOZEN FOR ME.

DID YOU HEAR? THIS IS THE SOLUTION TO ALL OUR PROBLEMS!

MASTER, I KNOW I TEND TO SCRAMBLE FOR THE EXIT ANY TIME YOU HATCH ANOTHER OF YOUR HALF-BOILED SCHEMES, BUT...

WITH THOSE EGGS I'LL BUY OFF THE ARMY AND BECOME CALIPH INSTEAD OF THE CALIPH!

4

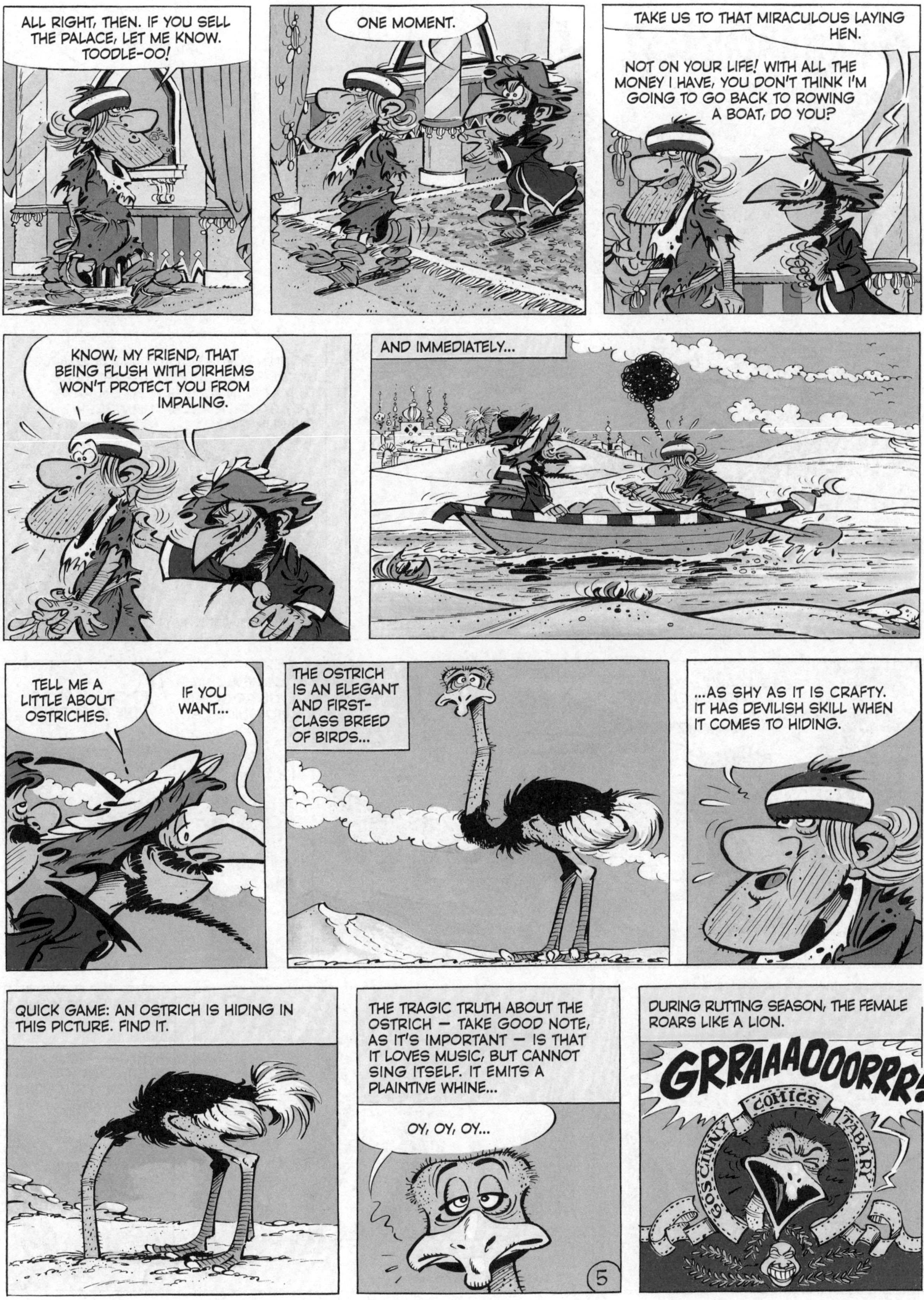
ALL RIGHT, THEN. IF YOU SELL THE PALACE, LET ME KNOW. TOODLE-OO!
ONE MOMENT.
TAKE US TO THAT MIRACULOUS LAYING HEN.
NOT ON YOUR LIFE! WITH ALL THE MONEY I HAVE, YOU DON'T THINK I'M GOING TO GO BACK TO ROWING A BOAT, DO YOU?
KNOW, MY FRIEND, THAT BEING FLUSH WITH DIRHEMS WON'T PROTECT YOU FROM IMPALING.
AND IMMEDIATELY...
TELL ME A LITTLE ABOUT OSTRICHES.
IF YOU WANT...
THE OSTRICH IS AN ELEGANT AND FIRST-CLASS BREED OF BIRDS...
...AS SHY AS IT IS CRAFTY. IT HAS DEVILISH SKILL WHEN IT COMES TO HIDING.
QUICK GAME: AN OSTRICH IS HIDING IN THIS PICTURE. FIND IT.
THE TRAGIC TRUTH ABOUT THE OSTRICH — TAKE GOOD NOTE, AS IT'S IMPORTANT — IS THAT IT LOVES MUSIC, BUT CANNOT SING ITSELF. IT EMITS A PLAINTIVE WHINE...
OY, OY, OY...
5
DURING RUTTING SEASON, THE FEMALE ROARS LIKE A LION.
GRRAAAOOORRR!
COMICS
GOSCINNY
TABARY

GRRAAAOOORRR!

!!!

OY, OY, OY.

WELL, WE'RE ALMOST THERE... OH, ONE LAST DETAIL...

THE RUINS OF THE CITY OF UR ARE GUARDED BY THE FIERCE CRUCIVERBALIST TRIBE. THEY LIVE IN BOXES, FEED ON RAYS THEY CATCH IN RILLS, AND WORSHIP THE SUN GOD RA.

YOU CAN'T MISS IT — IT'S STRAIGHT AHEAD.

COME ALONG. YOU'RE GOING TO GUIDE US.

TO-TAL-LY OUT OF THE QUESTION!

AFTER A LONG WALK...

HERE WE ARE... WE MUST LOOK FOR THE OSTRICH ... BUT DON'T MAKE A NOISE...

6

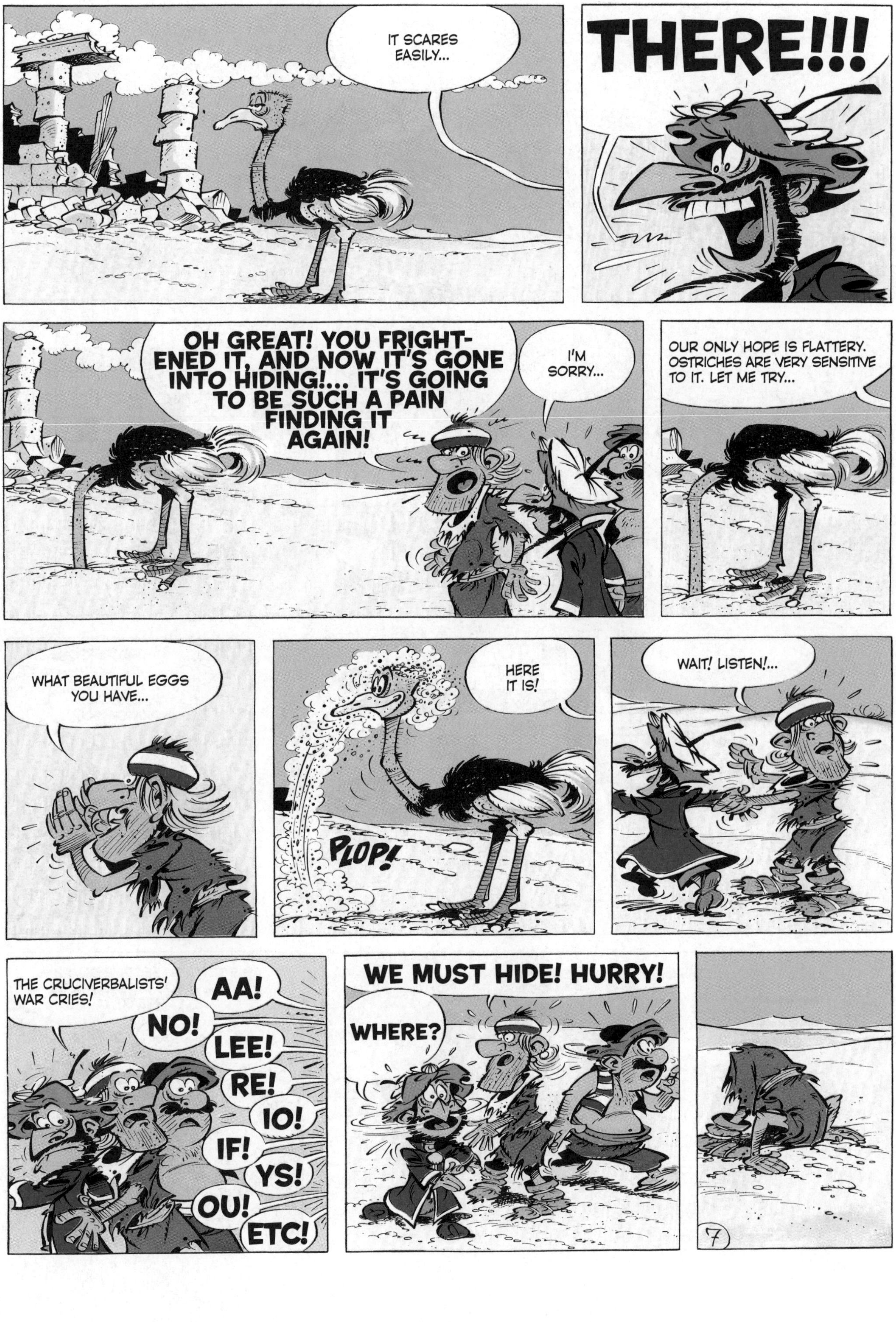
IT SCARES EASILY...
THERE!!!
OH GREAT! YOU FRIGHTENED IT, AND NOW IT'S GONE INTO HIDING!... IT'S GOING TO BE SUCH A PAIN FINDING IT AGAIN!
I'M SORRY...
OUR ONLY HOPE IS FLATTERY. OSTRICHES ARE VERY SENSITIVE TO IT. LET ME TRY...
WHAT BEAUTIFUL EGGS YOU HAVE...
HERE IT IS!
PLOP!
WAIT! LISTEN!...
THE CRUCIVERBALISTS' WAR CRIES!
AA!
NO!
LEE!
RE!
IO!
IF!
YS!
OU!
ETC!
WE MUST HIDE! HURRY!
WHERE?
7

LISTEN, LET ME EXPLAIN...

THESE SEIZE TWO MEN

WE WILL SACRIFICE THEM TONIGHT

THEY'RE GONE...

WHERE DID NOKATSH GO?

THERE!

I'LL BE! WHAT A CLEVER MAN!

AS SOON AS I BECOME CALIPH, I'LL GRANT YOU A REASONABLE TAX BREAK!

SHHH!

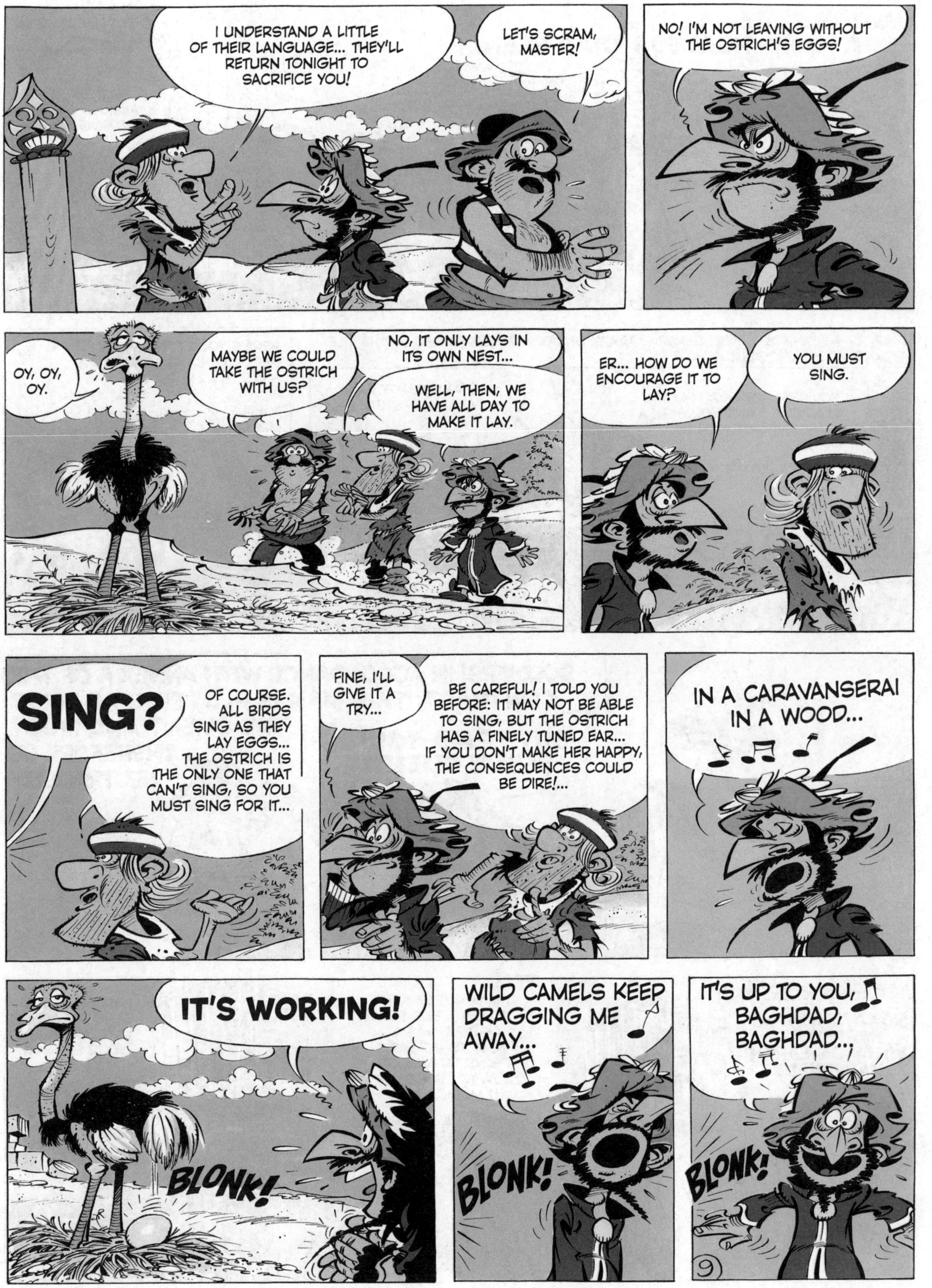
I UNDERSTAND A LITTLE OF THEIR LANGUAGE... THEY'LL RETURN TONIGHT TO SACRIFICE YOU!
LET'S SCRAM, MASTER!
NO! I'M NOT LEAVING WITHOUT THE OSTRICH'S EGGS!
OY, OY, OY.
MAYBE WE COULD TAKE THE OSTRICH WITH US?
NO, IT ONLY LAYS IN ITS OWN NEST...
WELL, THEN, WE HAVE ALL DAY TO MAKE IT LAY.
ER... HOW DO WE ENCOURAGE IT TO LAY?
YOU MUST SING.
SING?
OF COURSE. ALL BIRDS SING AS THEY LAY EGGS... THE OSTRICH IS THE ONLY ONE THAT CAN'T SING, SO YOU MUST SING FOR IT...
FINE, I'LL GIVE IT A TRY...
BE CAREFUL! I TOLD YOU BEFORE: IT MAY NOT BE ABLE TO SING, BUT THE OSTRICH HAS A FINELY TUNED EAR... IF YOU DON'T MAKE HER HAPPY, THE CONSEQUENCES COULD BE DIRE!...
IN A CARAVANSERAI IN A WOOD...
IT'S WORKING!
BLONK!
WILD CAMELS KEEP DRAGGING ME AWAY...
BLONK!
IT'S UP TO YOU, BAGHDAD, BAGHDAD...
BLONK!

SEVERAL HOURS LATER...

A HARD-HEADED HOURI BEEN...

BLONK!

OY, OY, OY.

OY, OY, OY.

I WISH THEY ALL COULD BE MESOPOTAMIA GIRLS...

MASTER, IT'S ALMOST NIGHT. WE HAVE TO GO.

AND SO, A FEW DAYS LATER, GENERAL ARASH UNPAK WAS SUMMONED BY THE VILE GRAND VIZIER IZNOGOUD...

SO, WE'RE AGREED: I PAY YOU IN ADVANCE AND YOU SIGN A CONTRACT WITH ME.

I STAND READY TO INITIAL AND SIGN.

HERE'S YOUR FIRST MISSION: DEPOSE AND ARREST CALIPH HAROUN AL PLASSID!

ONE MOMENT, PLEASE...

SOLDIERS! IN ACCORDANCE WITH ANNEX A OF THE CONTRACT, THIS MAN IS PLOTTING AGAINST THE CLIENT AND MUST THEREFORE BE NEUTRALISED!

BUT I PAID YOU! I'M THE CLIENT!

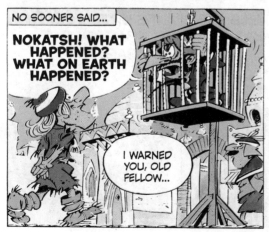

NO SOONER SAID...

NOKATSH! WHAT HAPPENED? WHAT ON EARTH HAPPENED?

I WARNED YOU, OLD FELLOW...

IT MAY NOT BE ABLE TO SING, BUT THE OSTRICH HAS A FINELY TUNED EAR... IT'S NEVER A GOOD IDEA TO DISPLEASE IT MUSICALLY...

SO, SINCE YOU SANG OFF-KEY, IT LAID FAKE EGGS. YOUR SERVANT, OLD BOY...